P9-DNT-888

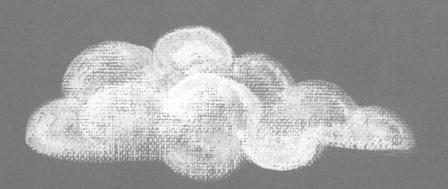

JUN — — 2009

Swing!

To Tia and Nonni

and in memory of Gary Hunt

Copyright © 2009 by Leslie Patricelli. All rights reserved. No part of this book may be reproduced, transmitted, or stored in an information retrieval system in any form or by any means, graphic, electronic, or mechanical, including photocopying, taping, and recording, without prior written permission from the publisher. First edition 2009. Library of Congress Cataloging-in-Publication Data is available. Library of Congress Catalog Card Number 2008935659. ISBN 978-0-7636-3241-0. Printed in China. This book was hand-lettered. The illustrations were done in acrylic. Candlewick Press, 99 Dover Street, Somerville, Massachusetts 02144. Visit us at www.candlewick.com. 10 9 8 7 6 5 4 3 2 1

Higher! Higher!

Leslie Patricelli

CANDLEWICK PRESS

Higher!

Higher! Higher!

five!

Bye!

Again!